Tall & Clumsy

ADELE K BATE

Tall & Clumsy

MOLLY & MUSTARD'S STORY PAD

Written and illustrated by
Adele K Bate

MOLLY & MUSTARD'S STORY PAD

Presenting: Gerard the giraffe,
the unlucky leading character, in this chaotic and clumsy tale.

In **Tall & Clumsy**, Gerard is having a sad and lonely time,
as nobody wants to hang out with a clumsy giraffe.
He goes in search of happiness, but guess what happens when
mishaps, marvel and mayhem, lead him to an unexpected place?

~ A message from AKB ~

To my devoted and unconditional support, Martin,
thanks for believing, always.

For all the busy mums out there,
dreams really can come true,
keep going and never give up!

Welcome to our story pad,
with interacting play,
you've chosen Tall and Clumsy,
to brighten up your day.

Now straighten up and settle down,
with your listening ears clicked on,
there's lots for you to read and learn,
following page one.

Your story begins with Gerard the giraffe,
the clumsiest guy around,
he was always tripping over things
and falling to the ground.

He'd stroll along the woodland path,
in search of juicy trees,
but before you could say clumsy,
he'd fall onto his knees.

Gerard's legs were the ones to blame
and sometimes bad luck too,
he tried not to be clumsy,
but he found it hard to do.
"You silly legs" Gerard sobbed,
in a sniveling gloomy tone,

"I wish I wasn't so clumsy" he thought,
"and I wish I wasn't alone".
It made him sad and it made him cry,
but what was he to do,
no-one wanted a clumsy friend,
so they hid and ran away too.

*iFACT: Did you know, giraffes come from the hot savanna areas of Africa and
are believed to have been on earth, for thirty to fifty million years?*

But then one day, Gerard woke and smiled up at the sky,
he said, "This week I won't be clumsy, if I really really try".

He scrunched his nose and shut his eyes,
praying for some good luck,

for some friends who really didn't mind,
when he became unstuck.

So off he went along the path and he found a quiet place,
"Hello" he said in a friendly voice, to a spider by his face.

But what poor Gerard hadn't seen, was a snail beside his feet,
he slid straight through its slimy trail, before he could retreat.

Poor old Gerard, what was he to do,
all he found here, was a slippery green goo!

iFACT: Did you know, giraffes love to eat the highest shoots and leaves of the thorny Acacia trees and use their long bristly haired tongues, to pull the leaves out?

The next day being Monday,
the path led to a green,
"Good morning" Gerard called out,
but the mole sat there was mean.

He laughed at Gerard sneezing
and when he kicked a snail's shell…

"Oh no", Gerard hollowed,
when the snail fell in the well.

Poor old Gerard,
he ignored the laughing mole,
and he ignored the laughing worm,
sat beside him in a hole.

*iFACT: Did you know, giraffes spend most of the day eating?
They can eat up to one hundred pounds of leaves and twigs a day, that's
around the same weight, as 16 heavy bricks.*

On Tuesday Gerard found a ball
and racket on the path,
and a busy little duck wash,
with a sail boat in a bath.

But soon he was in trouble,
he didn't have time to think,
he knocked the clothes dye in the basin
and turned the duck's hair pink.

Poor old Gerard, he said sorry eighteen times,

and he gave the duck two apples,
with a sandwich full of slime.

*iFACT: Did you know, giraffes are the tallest land mammals in the world?
They grow up to five meters tall, which can be as big as a house.*

On Wednesday Gerard bumped into, a prickly little guy,
he said, "I really like your roller-skates, can I have a try?"
The prickly guy said "Yes that's fine",
but Gerard sped out of control...

...he zoomed so fast his leg took flight
and he nearly hit the mole.

Poor old Gerard,
at first the mole was mean,
but as soon as Gerard scared him back,
he burrowed off the scene.

*iFACT: Did you know, giraffes can run up to thirty five miles per hour,
which is faster than a bus?*

Now Thursday Gerard saw a ladder,
leaning on a hut…

…and the laughing worm from Monday too,
who'd jammed his front door shut.

Gerard tried to help the worm,
by pulling at the door,
but suddenly the door flew off
and Gerard slid back on the floor.

Poor old Gerard, his tummy sank with fear,
he only tried to help the worm, who ended up in tears.

iFACT: Did you know, giraffes give birth to their baby calves whilst standing up? The calves are born up to two meters tall, around the same size as a door.

By Friday Gerard was all tired out,
so he stopped to have a rest,
he sat outside the mole's front door,
with his hooves upon his chest.

With an itch, a scratch and a shake of his tail,
an army of ants attacked...

…he was sat on top of their anthill
and the ants were demanding it back.

Poor old Gerard, he really didn't know,
until the angry ants evicted him
and told him where to go.

*iFACT: Did you know, giraffes sleep for less than two hours a day,
whilst kneeling or standing up?*

Well Saturday Gerard thought his luck,
was changing for the best,
he was asked to join a picnic,
but guess what happened next?

He skid straight through the picnic rug
and launched the milk up high,
"AHHH" the panicked guests all yelled,
when it soaked a prickly guy.

Poor old Gerard,
yet another clumsy mess,
he even spilt the juice jug
and the others weren't impressed.

iFACT: Did you know, giraffes can have up to twelve gallons of water in one drink, which is more than a bath full?

On Sunday Gerard left the path
and pitched his tent with pegs,
he built a fire and thought he'd have,
some bacon and fresh eggs.

He placed some bacon in the pan,
where it sizzled, hissed and popped,
but suddenly, the smoke grew wild
and Gerard couldn't make it stop.

Cough, cough, splutter, splutter,
poor Gerard could hardly see,
his hooves had totally disappeared,
when he fell back over a tree.

He'd tripped upon the open roots,
then his legs turned into jelly,
and when he tried to stand back up,
he tent surfed on his belly.

Poor old Gerard,
what a way to end his week,
of seven clumsy days
and the worst unlucky streak.

*iFACT: Did you know, giraffes have four stomachs and are known
as ruminant animals? This means, like cows, they have
more than one stomach to help digest their food.*

With a flattened tent and bacon burnt,
poor Gerard could take no more,
when he heard a breaking branches noise,
behind the tent's front doors.

The prickly guys appeared,
with the mole, duck and Ted,
they all looked terribly frightened,
as they wandered out of bed.

"Hello" said Gerard a little surprised,
"what are you doing here?"
"Spooky noises" cried a prickly guy,
whose face was filled with fear.

"Would you like to share my camp?"
Gerard answered back,
"and you could share my cup of Cocoa,
but my bacon's burnt and black".

iFACT: Did you know, giraffes have two lumps on their heads called ossicones?
The ossicones protect the males when they fight over a female,
in a show of strength, this is called 'necking'.

"That's really kind" said the worm,
appearing from his hole,
"and thoughtful" squealed the prickly guy,
beside the frightened mole.
They followed Gerard down the hill,
"Sit here", he softly said,

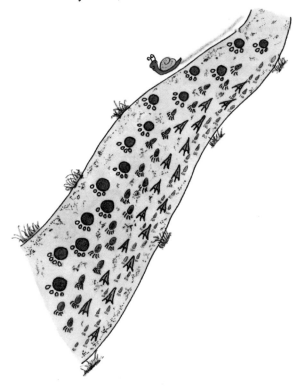

where he gathered them round the camp fire
and made up stories from his head.
With all ears and eyes upon him,
not a whisper could be heard,
just Gerard's gentle voice
and the magic from his words.

He spoke of hidden treasure and pirates by the sea,
a wizard and a dragon, then a princess and a pea.
But when he'd told his final tale, he saw their sleepy eyes,
he said, "Good night sweet dreams, my new found friends,
it's time for beddy-byes".

And so the group all made their way, back over to the wood,
but this time they were smiling, as Gerard's stories were so good.

*iFACT: Did you know, giraffes can live up to twenty five years old in the wild
and can weigh more than 2000 kilograms? That's as heavy, as an ice-cream van.*

They realised that sometimes people
can't help what they do,

and that anyone can be clumsy,
even me and you!

Now everyone loves Gerard
and they turn a blind eye when he falls,
when he knocks and tips and spills things,
and walks into garden walls.

So if you ever see him stumble,
just think twice before you laugh,
because although Gerard's rather clumsy,
he's a wonderful Giraffe.

iFACT: Did you know, a giraffe's tongue can grow up to 50cm long?
That's longer than your elbow, to your finger tips.

So we've reached the end and you've listened well,
to this Tall and Clumsy tale,

from roller-skating acrobats,
to sneezes and flying snails.

We hope you liked our story pad,
with learning along the way,

and now it's time to say goodbye,
but please come back one day.

iFACTS: *Return to the beginning for interesting* **FACTS**,
on the tallest animal in the world.

Adele Bate was born in Manchester,
leaving school with a modest amount of GCSE's.
With the lure of London proving irresistible, Adele undertook a short spell
working in the capital, followed by a stint of travel in Oz.
Eventually Adele settled back in her home city of Manchester, starting a family,
where she juggles her love of writing, work and 3 lively children.

As well as her debut release Tall & Clumsy, Adele is busy working on the second
installment from Molly & Mustard's Story Pad, titled 'Mummy's Growing Tummy'. In a
heartwarming interpretation, the story takes you on a special journey through the eyes
of her toddler and prepares young siblings, in welcoming a new baby to their family.

Visit www.adelebate.com for a flavor of Adele's journey and upcoming News.

ISBN-13: 978-1979456777
ISBN-10: 1979456771

Printed by CreateSpace
Available from Amazon.com and other retail outlets

Printed in Great Britain
by Amazon